A Pet

The Sound of P

By Alice K. Flanagan

The Child's World®

I took my pack.

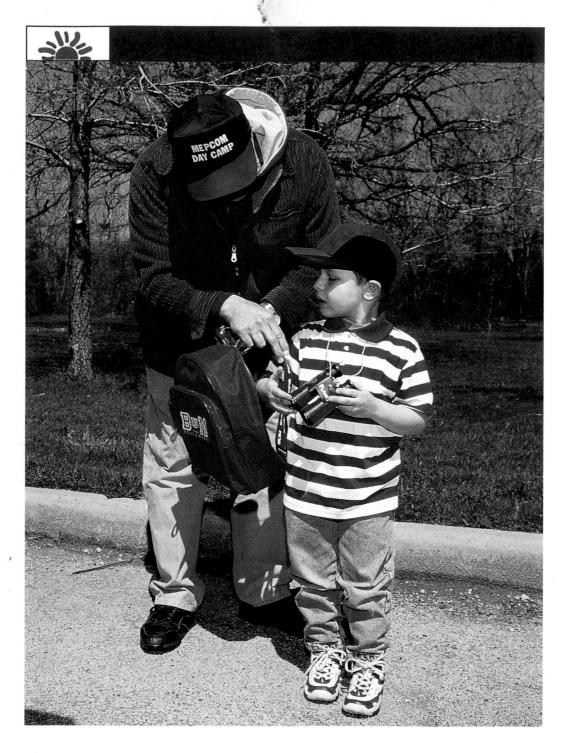

I put my pack on my back.

I went to find a pet.

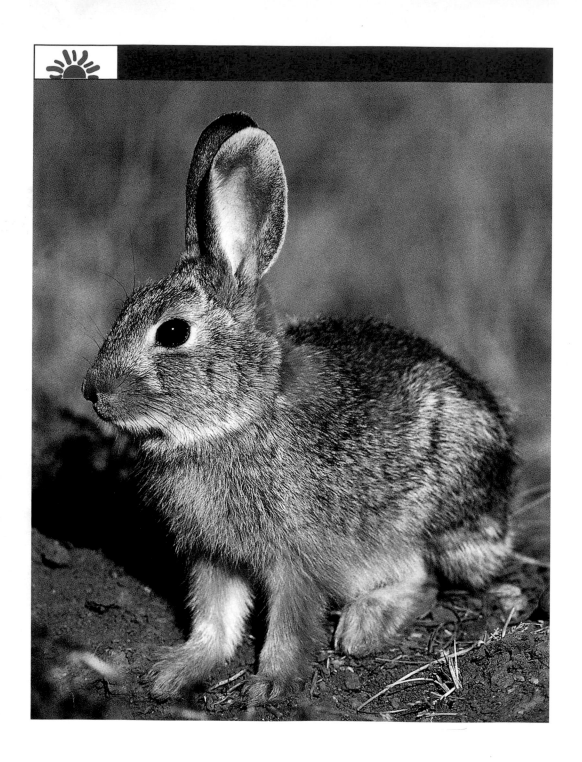

I met a pet on the path.

I met a pet in a pen.

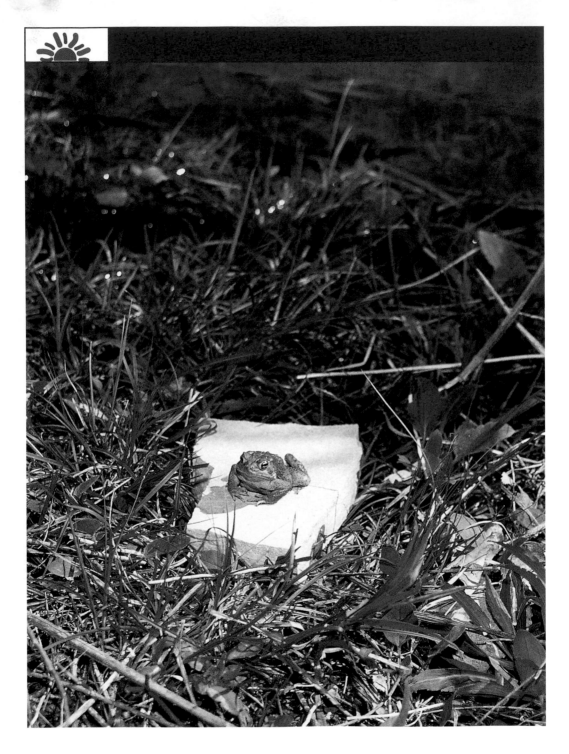

I met a pet at the pond.

I picked a pet for
my pal.

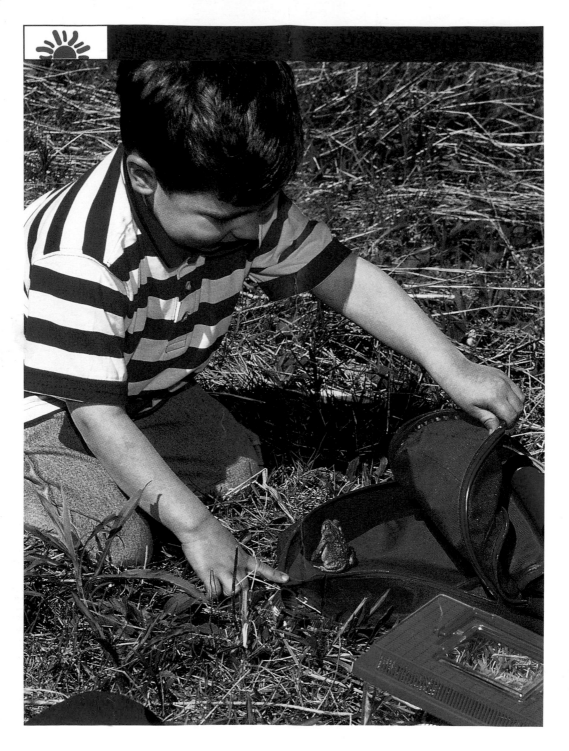

He jumped into my pack.

We took a walk.

We had a talk.

My pal and I are friends.

Word List

pack	pet
pal	picked
path	pond
pen	put

Note to Parents and Educators

Welcome to Wonder Books® Phonics Readers! These books are based on current research that supports the idea that our brains detect patterns rather than apply rules. This means that children learn to read more easily when they are taught the familiar spelling patterns found in English. As children progress in their reading, they can use these spelling patterns to figure out more complex words.

The Phonics Readers texts provide the opportunity to practice and apply knowledge of the sounds in natural language. The ten books on the long and short vowels introduce the sounds using familiar onsets and *rimes*, or spelling patterns, for reinforcement. The letter(s) before the vowel in a word are considered the onset. Changing the onset allows the consonant books in the series to maintain the practice and reinforcement of the rimes. The repeated use of a word or phrase reinforces the target sound.

As an example, the word "cat" might be used to present the short "a" sound, with the letter "c" being the onset and "–at" being the rime. This approach provides practice and reinforcement for the short "a" sound, since there are many familiar words with the "–at" rime.

The number on the spine of each book facilitates arranging the books in the order in which the sounds are learned. The books can also be arranged into groups of long vowels, short vowels, consonants, and blends. All the books in each grouping have their numbers printed in the same color on the spine. The books can be grouped and regrouped easily and quickly, depending on the teacher's needs.

The stories and accompanying photographs in this series are based on time-honored concepts in children's literature: Well-written, engaging texts and colorful, high-quality photographs combine to produce books that children want to read again and again.

Dr. Peg Ballard
Minnesota State University, Mankato, MN

About the Author

Alice K. Flanagan taught elementary school for ten years. Now she writes for children and teachers. She has been writing for more than twenty years. Some of her books include biographies, phonics books, holiday books, and information books about careers, animals, and weather. Alice K. Flanagan lives with her husband in Chicago, Illinois.

Photo Credits

All photos © copyright: Romie Flanagan/Flanagan Publishing Services, except 8 (Dembinsky Photo Assoc./Stan Osolinski) and 11 (Dembinsky Photo Assoc./Dusty Perin). Cover photo © Romie Flanagan/Flanagan Publishing Services.

Special thanks to Gnadt family

Photo Research: Alice Flanagan
Design and production: Herman Adler Design Group

Library of Congress Cataloging-in-Publication Data

Flanagan, Alice K.
    A Pet : The sound of "p" / by Alice K. Flanagan.
      p. cm. — (Wonder books)
    Summary : Simple text and repetition of the letter "p" help readers learn how to use this sound.
    ISBN 1-56766-687-6 (lib. bdg. : alk. paper)
    [1. Alphabet.] I. Title. II. Series: Wonder books (Chanhassen, Minn.)
PZ7.F59824Pe   1999
[E]—dc21
                                              99-20955
                                               CIP